Jack and the Beanstalk

Once upon a time, in a little village far, far away, there was a boy named Jack. He lived in a tiny cottage with his mother. They were very poor, but Jack loved his mother dearly and they worked hard every day to make ends meet.

Their only possession was an old cow that Jack milked every morning. After gathering the day's milk, he and his mother would head to the market and sell the milk. Then, they would buy food with their earnings. One day, the tired old cow couldn't give any more milk.

Without any money or food, Jack and his mother had no choice but to sell their poor cow. Jack's mother asked him to take the cow to the market and sell her to the highest bidder. Jack was sad to have to get rid of their beloved friend, but he did as his mother told him.

4

On his way to the market, Jack passed a butcher shop. When he saw Jack, the butcher rushed out of his shop.

"Well, hello there, Jack! How much for that cow?" asked the butcher politely.

Jack shrugged. "As much as I can get," he said. "My mother and I need money to buy food."

The butcher reached into his pocket and pulled out five beans.

"What if I trade you these magic beans instead?" he said.
"Plant these beans, and I guarantee you'll have all the money
you'll ever need by morning!"

Curious, Jack accepted the offer and hurried home to tell his mother. When he showed the beans to his mother, she was furious.

"That cow was all we had!" she shouted. "You traded her for these worthless beans?"

With that, she tossed the beans out the window, and sent Jack to bed without supper.

The next morning, Jack awoke in a dark room. Something huge was blocking his window! He got out of bed and discovered that a giant beanstalk had grown in the spot where his mother had thrown the beans! He dressed quickly and rushed outside to inspect the mighty plant.

He could see no end to the beanstalk, so Jack decided to climb it to see how high it reached. He climbed up, up, up, and was soon surrounded by clouds. His cottage was nothing more than a tiny speck below him. There was no turning back now! He bravely climbed higher and higher until he reached the very top of the stalk.

At the top, Jack hopped down onto a cloudy floor. The first thing he saw was a great castle adorned in gold and jewels. The castle was so big that Jack figured it must belong to a giant… a very rich giant!

Jack knocked on the humongous door.

It wasn't long before a lady opened the door. She was the giant's wife, and a very kind woman. She invited Jack inside for lunch.

As Jack ate, he heard heavy footsteps coming down the hall.

"That's my husband!" the wife exclaimed. "He doesn't take kindly to people. Quick, hide in the kettle!"

The giant's voice boomed angrily. "Fee, fi, fo, fum, I smell the blood of an Englishman!"

"Nonsense!" the giant's wife replied. "There's no Englishman anywhere here!"

She carried the kettle to the kitchen counter, out of the giant's reach.

Jack sat inside the kettle and listened intently.

Just then, the giant's voice roared again.

"Bring me my chest!" he said to his wife. "I want to count my gold!"

As he counted his gold coins, the giant got very tired. He fell asleep, snoring loudly. Jack saw his chance to escape. He climbed out of the kettle and grabbed the bags of coins.

Jack hopped down off the table with his treasure and scurried toward the door. It was only open a crack and he just barely managed to squeeze through.

Just as he neared the beanstalk, Jack heard a rumble of heavy footsteps. The giant was in the castle doorway!

"Someone stole my gold!" he roared. "When I find him, I'll make him pay!"

The giant looked to the left and to the right. He spotted Jack and charged toward the beanstalk with big strides.

Jack tied the sacks of gold to his belt and hopped onto the stalk. He shimmied downward as quickly as he could. He was moving fast, but not fast enough! The giant had already reached the beanstalk!

The giant began to chase Jack. The beanstalk swayed back and forth under their weight. The giant was not nearly as quick as Jack and had trouble keeping the beanstalk steady enough to climb. Jack was a very nimble boy and easily scaled the rest of the way down.

Jack hopped off the beanstalk and ran straight into the house to grab an ax. Jack chopped furiously at the thick beanstalk. The giant was gaining speed, and was now halfway down the stalk.

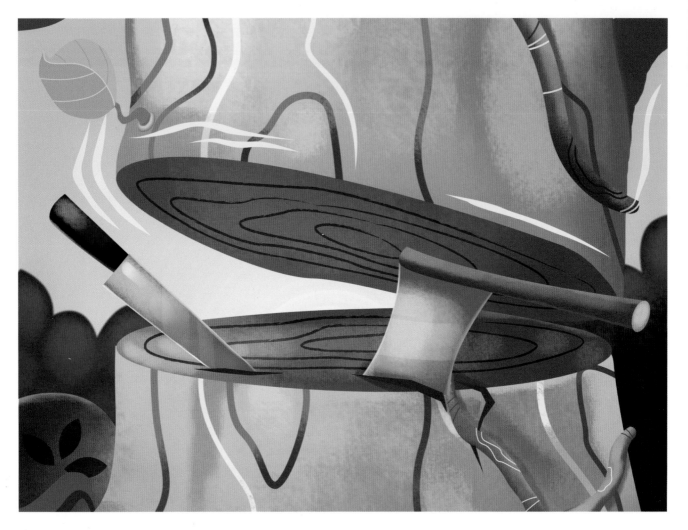

Jack chopped and chopped until his arms were sore. Just then, his mother appeared.

"Mother, help me cut down this stalk. There's a giant chasing me!"

His mother fetched a kitchen knife, and together they chopped halfway through the stalk.

The stalk began to shake under the giant's weight. Suddenly, there was a loud snap! The stalk cracked and the mighty plant came crashing to the ground… and so did the giant! Jack had defeated him!

"What's going on?" Jack's mother asked.

Jack told his mother the incredible story of the magic beanstalk, the castle, and the giant. At the very end of the tale, he revealed his bags of gold coins.

"We'll never go hungry again, Mother!" Jack said proudly.

Jack's mother jumped for joy. She hugged her beloved son and they immediately went to the market to buy food and supplies. They also bought a new cow, so they could continue to sell milk at the market.

Jack and his mother were never in need again. They worked hard on their farm and never had to wish for any more money. Together, they lived happily ever after.